THE SLEEP PONIES

Written and Illustrated by Gudrun Geibel Ongman

MINDCASTLE BOOKS

Woodinville

Thanks first to my daughters, Mara, Lissa, and Carly and their pony Whinny. The indelible memories of their play were my ever-enchanting models for the artwork. Thanks to the many friends, artists and students who provided encouragement and critique throughout the evolution of *The Sleep Ponies*. Special gratitude is due Liana Bennett, Jeanene MacKinnon and Vanessa Jensen. Thank you to Cheryl Hadley for invaluable expertise in editing. And last but never least to my husband Jim, for his nearly limitless support and patience.

Text and illustrations copyright © 2000 by Gudrun Geibel Ongman.
Published by:
MindCastle™ Books, Inc.
P.O. Box 3005
Woodinville, Washington 98072
www.mindcastle.com

The text is set in Garamond and the illustrations are rendered in watercolor and pastel.
Designer: Chris Lassen

10 9 8 7 6 5 4
Printed in Korea

Library of Congress Cataloging in Publication Data
Ongman, Gudrun.
    The sleep ponies/written and illustrated by
Gudrun Ongman. --1st ed.
    p.cm.
    SUMMARY: Grandma teaches a young girl how to
call sleep ponies to ride with her in dreams at
night.
    LCCN:00-90088
    ISBN:0-9677204-0-0

    1. Ponies--Juvenile fiction. 2. Dreams--
Juvenile fiction. 3. Sleep--Juvenile fiction.
I. Title.
PZ7.O562S1 2000   [E]
                                   QBI00-159

For my mother and the ponies she introduced
me to so many years ago.
And for the children who learn to call them.

My grandma told me whenever you
  want them, sleep ponies are near.
  Her mother taught her to call them
  when she was little.

"Teach *me*, grandma.

  Teach me to call *my* ponies,"
I begged.

She paused and remembered,

"Through closed eyes you see them.
In silence you hear them.
In stillness you touch them."

I squirmed with excitement.

"You'll need to be very patient,"
she whispered.

"I can do it," I promised,
"I can do it," I hoped.

"Then hush now, be ever so still.
Only your heart can call them."

"When dust dances in patches of light.

When your soft pillow muffles
    the sounds of the house.

When your breathing slows and
    mist floats behind your closed eyes,

listen for them,
    call silently to them."

"Listen for a distant nicker,
    and the faint sound of hooves.
    Find the round smell of pony."

Grandma smiled, then continued,
    "Watch the mist brighten
    and shift to let one pony
    step quietly through."

I lay still and silent,
my eyes closed.

Just as Grandma promised, my pony Whinny appeared.

And just as Grandma warned, when I reached out or opened my eyes, she vanished.

So I remembered to hold ever so still, and open my heart instead of my eyes, and reach out with love instead of hands.

Fuzzy, round little Whinny
returned to step closer.

When she came close enough for
me to feel her warm breath, we
talked without words.

Her invitation to ride flowed
from the depths of her
kind eyes.

"Yes," my heart-hands answered as they
wove deep into silky mane and pulled me
aboard her sturdy, round back.

Instantly bright sunshine
and golden grass surrounded us.
A herd of wild ponies nearby watched me expectantly.

My eyes skipped over their coats of copper and gold, chocolate
and snow, and slid down their manes and tails from
spotted hide to stockinged hoof.

I paused on a face with a blaze,

and moved on to one with a star.

At my nod, we were off!

Warm pony below, warm sun above.

What joy to ride along with that little band.

At first Whinny picked her steps and
shifted her body to keep me balanced.

But soon I was riding with the wind,
    a part of the herd as we galloped along,
        leaping a bush here, dodging a stone there,

and splashing through sparkling streams.

At last,
        we slowed to a walk.

My ponies taught me to breathe the scent of each colorful flower
        and to gather the sounds of birds who hid among the grasses
        and followed gaily through the air.

I learned to greet each rabbit, chipmunk and fox.
        And to thank the clouds for their cool shadows drifting by.

As the herd munched lush grass and swished long tails,
    I stretched out on Whinny's back.

Full of sound and smell and sight,
    we shared stories and daydreams.

Then we yawned
            and sighed,

glad a resting place was near.

We moved slowly and quietly
toward the pond,

a magical place

where sweet breezes called from the leaves of shade trees.
Frogs croaked hello. And the water itself shivered
ripples of excitement at our approach.

Kneeling in damp moss,
I quenched my thirst with cupped hands,

while Whinny dipped her muzzle
into the cool water.

As shimmering waves carried
off our reflections,

my eyelids grew heavy.

Soon Whinny led me to a special place
where moss grew thick and firm.

As we lay down, I nestled so close
against her shoulder and into her neck
that it was hard to see

where I ended
and she began.

My eyes closed as I heard the other ponies lying down.
My fingers wandered through the long strands of her mane.
The slow steady beating of Whinny's heart mingled with my own.

Together we slept.

Much later the ponies lifted and carried me home
so quietly and so carefully that I never awoke...

Until I was back in my bed surrounded by
    the sweet scent of pony

and a smile.